MUM!
THE
MONSTERS!

Written by
Liliana Cinetto

Illustrated by
Poly Bernatene

For my children Sol, Juani y Flor,
because in fact they are the ones
who really protect me.

L.C.

For Matias and his curls!
And to Mom Paula, who protects
us from the monsters.

P. B.

This edition published by Parragon in 2013
Parragon
Chartist House
15-17 Trim Street
Bath BA1 1HA, UK
www.parragon.com

Published by arrangement with Meadowside Children's Books
185 Fleet Street, London, EC4A 2HS

Text © Liliana Cinetto 2011
Illustrations © Poly Bernatene 2011

ISBN 978-1-4723-3434-3

Printed in China

MUM! THE MONSTERS!

Written by
Liliana Cinetto

Illustrated by
Poly Bernatene

PaRragon

Bath · New York · Singapore · Hong Kong · Cologne · Delhi
Melbourne · Amsterdam · Johannesburg · Shenzhen

Once upon a time, I was very, very afraid at night. Terribly afraid.

So afraid that my hands shook like this...

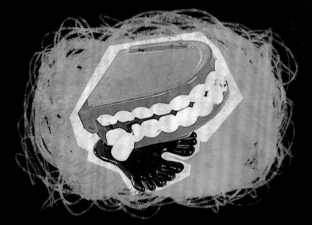

And my teeth chattered like this...

And my heart beat like this...

I was afraid because I thought that THEY
were hiding in the dark. Hairy monsters with
sharp teeth who smelled of dirty socks.

And then there
was THEM.

Dreadful ghosts
floating in the air
trailing dust
and cobwebs.

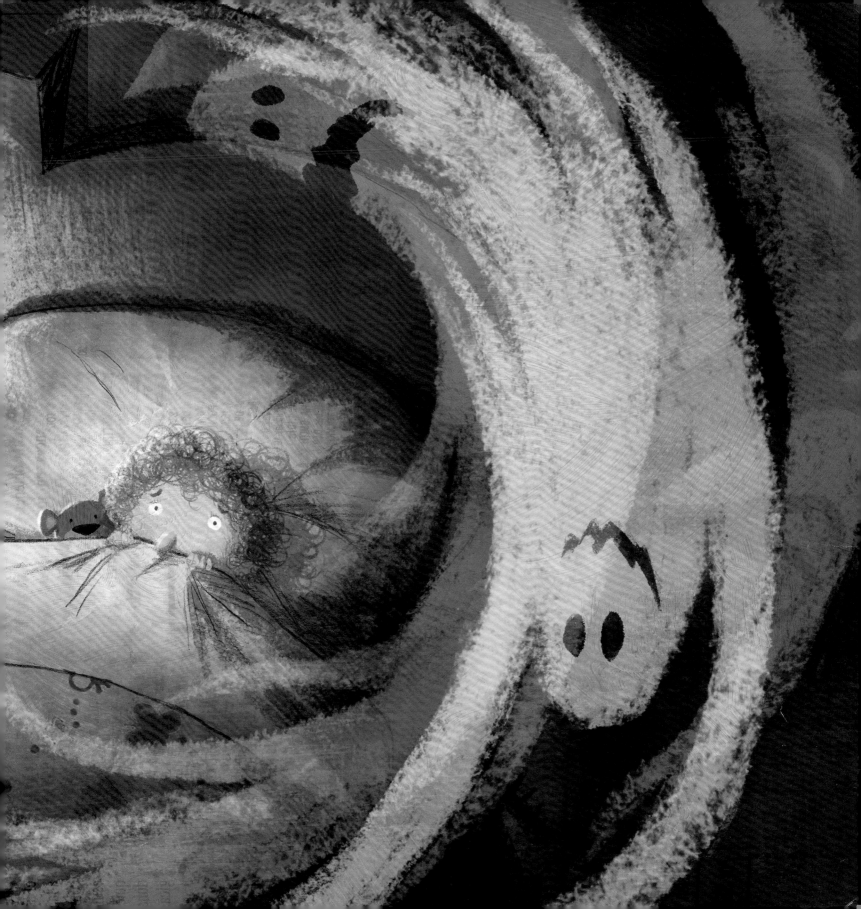

Or THEM.

Witches with messy
hair and black hats
and yellow eyes.

Or even THEM.

Huge ogres with huge hands and huge
feet and huge mouths full of
green drool.

I was sure that they wanted to catch me. Or turn
me into a toad. Or eat me with a sprinkling of parsley.
So, in the middle of the night, I'd shout:

"Muuuuuuum! The monsters!"

And Mum would
put on the light
and sing songs to
me until I went
back to sleep.

And, in a dark corner, the monsters and the witches
and the ghosts and the ogres waited.
They did not move.

But they were watching me...

Then, one day, Mum got tired of
always having to get up in the
middle of the night.
"You're a big boy now. You shouldn't
be afraid any more."

"But Mum, the monsters..."
"Monsters don't exist," she said, as she vacuumed under
my bed, sucking up the dust and some hairy monsters
(the ones with sharp teeth who smelled of dirty socks).

"What about the ghosts?" I asked.
"They don't exist either," she said, as she loaded
the washing machine with towels and sheets
and a few dreadful ghosts

(the ones who floated
about trailing dust
and cobwebs).

"But what about
the witches?" I asked.
"Not at all," she told
me while she tidied up the
cupboard, straightening
the books and a few witches
(the ones with messy hair
and black hats and yellow eyes).

"And the
ogres?"
I wanted
to know.

"No way!" said Mum as she swept the kitchen floor, brushing up breadcrumbs and bits of paper and a few huge ogres (the ones with huge hands, huge feet and huge mouths full of green drool).

"Are you sure, Mum?
Are there really
no monsters?"

"They're just stories dear!" she told me
while she washed up the plates and the monsters...

...and ironed the sheets and the ghosts...

And while she
cleaned the furniture
and the witches...

And had a rest on the sofa with some comfy cushions and huge ogres.

That's why I'm not scared
of anything now.
Monsters, ghosts, witches
and ogres don't come to my
bedroom any more:
THEY are too afraid!

Because they know that their biggest
nightmare lives in my house...

...my mum!

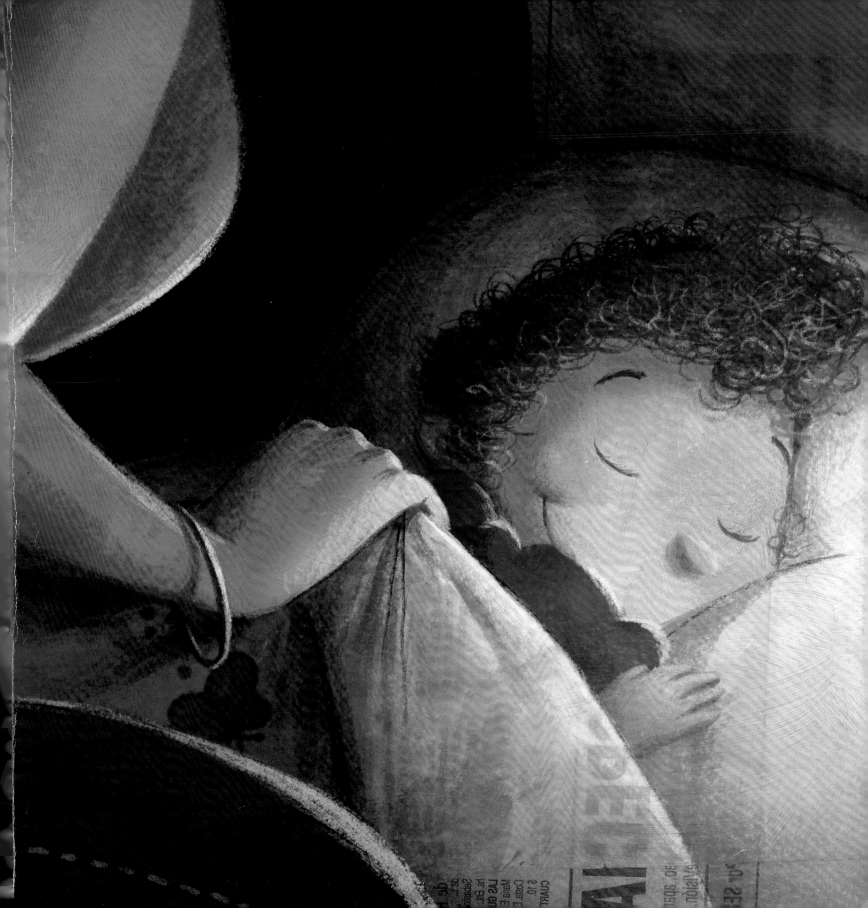